Mirandy and Brother Wind

by Patricia C. McKissack

Illustrated by Jerry Pinkney

Alfred A. Knopf New York

Remembering—Miranda and Moses P.C.M.

For Myles, Sandra, and my grandson, Leon J.P.

This is a Borzoi Book published by Alfred A. Knopf, Inc.

Text copyright © 1988 by Patricia C. McKissack.
Illustrations copyright © 1988 by Jerry Pinkney.
All rights reserved under International and Pan-American Copyright
Conventions. Published in the United States by Alfred A. Knopf, Inc.,
New York, and simultaneously in Canada by Random House of Canada
Limited, Toronto. Distributed by Random House, Inc., New York.
Manufactured in the United States of America
Book design by Mina Greenstein
10

Library of Congress Cataloging-in-Publication Data
McKissack, Patricia, 1944– . Mirandy and Brother Wind.
Summary: To win first prize in the Junior Cakewalk, Mirandy tries to
capture the wind for her partner. [1. Dancing—Fiction.
2. Winds—Fiction. 3. Afro-Americans—Fiction] I. Pinkney,
Jerry, ill. II. Title. PZ7.M478693Mi 1988 [E] 87-349
ISBN 0-394-88765-4 ISBN 0-394-98765-9 (lib. bdg.)

AUTHOR'S NOTE

One of our family treasures is a rare picture of my grandparents dated 1906, five years before they were married. They were teenagers at the time and had just won a cakewalk. As winners, they'd been awarded an elaborately decorated cake.

First introduced in America by slaves, the cakewalk is a dance rooted in Afro-American culture. It was performed by couples who strutted and pranced around a large square, keeping time with fiddle and banjo music. As the dancers paraded by, doing flamboyant kicks and complicated swirls and turns, the elders judged them on appearance, grace, precision, and originality of moves. The winning couple took home a cake.

It's never been difficult for me to imagine my grandparents strutting around a square with their backs arched, their toes pointed, and their heads held high. . . . They were full of life's joy, especially Mama. Papa used to say he believed Mama had captured the Wind. I believed it too.

Patricia C. McKissack

Swish! Swish!

It was spring, and Brother Wind was back. He come high steppin' through Ridgetop, dressed in his finest and trailing that long, silvery wind cape behind him.

Swoosh! Swoosh! Swoosh!

"Sure wish Brother Wind could be my partner at the junior cakewalk tomorrow night," say Mirandy, her face pressed against the cool cabin window. "Then I'd be sure to win."

Ma Dear smiled. "There's an old saying that whoever catch the Wind can make him do their bidding."

"I'm goin' to," say Mirandy. And she danced around the room, dipping, swinging, turning, wheeling. "This is my first cakewalk. And I'm gon' dance with the Wind!"

When the sky turned morning pink, Mirandy set out to capture Brother Wind. Grandmama Beasley was out back feeding her chickens when Mirandy come up asking all excited, "Do you know how to catch Brother Wind? I want to make him be my partner at the cakewalk tonight."

Grandmama Beasley studied on the notion. "Can't nobody put shackles on Brother Wind, chile. He be special. He be free."

Mirandy asked all her neighbors the same question, but nobody seemed to have an answer.

"I'm gon' get him yet," she say, turning 'round and 'round in the yard.

"Get who?"

She didn't even have to look around to know it was that clumsy boy Ezel. Mirandy didn't answer but walked toward the road. Ezel came too, walking backward to face her. He was sure to trip any minute. And he did.

"Why you been asking everybody how to catch the Wind?"

"Ma Dear tol' me whoever catch the Wind can make him do their bidding. I want him to be my partner at the cakewalk tonight."

"But I thought I . . ." After a moment Ezel flashed his good-natured smile. His eyes sparkled like sun glints on branch water. He say, "What do you think Orlinda would say if I asked her to be my partner?"

"Orlinda! Skinny Orlinda! Ask her and find out," say Mirandy, and she strutted away.

At the corner store Mr. Jessup told Mirandy that a great-aunt of his from Ipsala, Mississippi, said to put black pepper in Brother Wind's footprints. That would make him sneeze. "While he's busy sneezing, slip up behind and throw a quilt over him."

Mirandy rushed home and got the black-pepper mill and one of Ma Dear's quilts. Wasn't long 'fore Brother Wind came strolling through the meadow, his wind cape hovering gentle-like over the grasses.

Sneaking up behind him, Mirandy commenced to grinding pepper. Then she threw the quilt. But—*whoosh!* Brother Wind was gone.

Mirandy was still sneezing when she told Ezel what happened.

"I could have tol' you the Wind don't leave footprints," he say as he milked the family cow. He was sure to spill some. And he did.

Mirandy sneezed again.

"Did you ask Orlinda 'bout being your partner?" she say, changing the subject.

"Sure did, and she said—"

"I don't care what she said," Mirandy interrupted, and rushed away.

Following the creek downstream, Mirandy come to Mis Poinsettia's whitewashed cottage. Talk had it that Mis Poinsettia wasn't a for-real conjure woman like the ones in New Orleans. But didn't nobody mess with her, just in case talk was wrong.

Mis Poinsettia welcomed Mirandy inside. "Your people don't approve of conjure. Why come you here?" she say.

Mirandy figured if Mis Poinsettia was up on her conjure she ought to know why. But not wanting to 'pear sassy, she answered, "I need a potion to help me catch Brother Wind so he'll be my partner at the cakewalk."

The woman shook her head. Then she switched over to a cupboard, her jewelry jingling and jangling and the colorful scarves sewn to her dress fluttering about.

In a quick minute she returned with an ol' book. Mirandy put the words in her head as Mis Poinsettia read them.

"I'm ever grateful," say Mirandy. "But all I have as payment are my Christmas and birthday nickels."

"Consider me well paid if you wear these when you dance tonight. And I guarantee you'll be the prettiest girl there." And Mis Poinsettia gave Mirandy two of her see-through scarves.

Mirandy hurried home. Like the conjure spell said, she found a crock bottle . . . washed it in water from the rain barrel . . . and poured in a measure of cider. Then she made her way to the big willow down by the branch and set the bottle on the tree's north side. Nothing left to do but wait.

'Fore long Brother Wind come out the woods. Mirandy had never seen a body stand so tall or hold his head so high. The conjure was working. He smelled the cider. With a big *whoosh* he jumped into the bottle.

"I got you!" Mirandy pushed in the cork and danced 'round and 'round. But when she looked, Brother Wind was on the other side of the branch, bent over laughing. Then, flicking the tail of the wind cape, he vanished. *Swoosh!*

"How did he get in and out of that bottle so fast?" she asked Ezel at the woodpile. He'd pulled the wrong log, and the whole pile had come crashing down on him. Mirandy was helping him restack it. "What am I gon' do?"

Ezel laughed. "Looks like you gon' need a partner."

Mirandy got purely upset. "You laughing, but just wait! I'll catch him yet!" she shouted, and left in a huff.

The cakewalk was only a few hours away, and Mirandy was moping on the front porch swing when Brother Wind swooped over the hedges, kicking up dust. He leaped over the lilacs, around the snowball tree, and into the barn.

While he was inside shaking the rafters and scaring Ma Dear's hens, Mirandy slipped up quiet-like and slammed the door. No way for him to get out, 'cause Pa had stuffed all the cracks.

"I got you!" she say, clapping her hands. "Now you've got to do whatever I ask."

At dusk the neighbors from the Ridge started gathering at the schoolhouse, everybody dressed in their Sunday best. The fiddlers stood in one corner, and Grandmama Beasley and the other elder folk sat in the judges' seats. Elder Thomas brought in two big triple-decker cakes—one for the junior cakewalk winners and the other for the grown-up winners. Somebody drew a big square in the middle of the floor, and the cakewalk jubilee began.

First thing, Orlinda come siding up to Mirandy, asking, "Who gon' be yo' partner?"

Mirandy tried not to act excited. "He's real special." Then she added, "I wish you and Ezel luck. Y'all gon' need it."

"Me and Ezel? Girl, don't be silly. He asked, but I wouldn't dance with that ol' clumsy boy for nothing," she say, fanning herself. "Why, he can't even now walk and breathe at the same time. I didn't want him tripping over my feet in front of the whole county." And the girls laughed.

Mirandy put her hands on her hips and moved right in close to Orlinda. "You just hush making fun of Ezel, you hear?" she say quiet-like. "He's my friend, and it just so happens *we're* gon' win that cake!" And she tossed her head in the air and hurried away.

Outside Mirandy wondered why she'd said such a tomfool thing. She'd caught Brother Wind. Ezel couldn't be her partner. But an idea came.

"Brother Wind," she called. "You still in there?" The barn door rattled and almost shook off its hinges. "I'm ready with my wish." She whispered it, then hurried to find Ezel.

Weeks passed, and still Ridge folk talked 'bout how Mirandy and Ezel had won the junior cakewalk. That night they'd pranced 'round and 'round, cutting corners with style and grace. *Swish! Swish!* And when the music had changed to a fast gait, they'd arched their backs, kicked up their heels, and reeled from side to side. *Swoosh! Swoosh!*

Folk still talked about how Mirandy was a picture of pretty, dressed in yellow with two colorful scarves tied 'round each wrist. And everybody agreed Ezel had never stood taller or held his head higher.

When Grandmama Beasley had seen Mirandy and Ezel turning and spinning, moving like shadows in the flickering candlelight, she'd thrown back her head, laughed, and said, "Them chullin' is dancing with the Wind!"